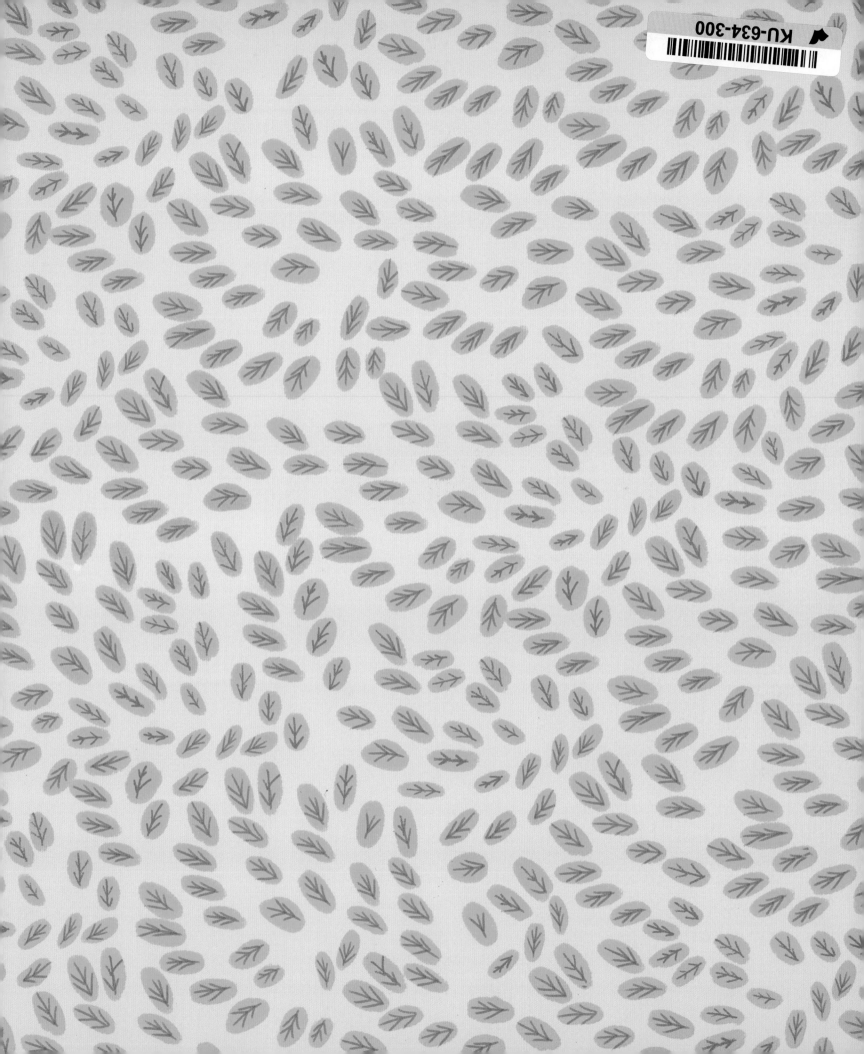

*For Edwyn and Stanley*
~ L S


*For Grandma Tickle*
~ J C-T

LITTLE TIGER PRESS LTD,
an imprint of the Little Tiger Group
1 Coda Studios, 189 Munster Road, London SW6 6AW
www.littletiger.co.uk

First published in Great Britain 2019
This edition published 2020

A CIP catalogue record for this book is available from the British Library

Printed in China • LTP/1400/2948/1019

2 4 6 8 10 9 7 5 3 1

This Little Tiger book
belongs to:

_____

_____

_____

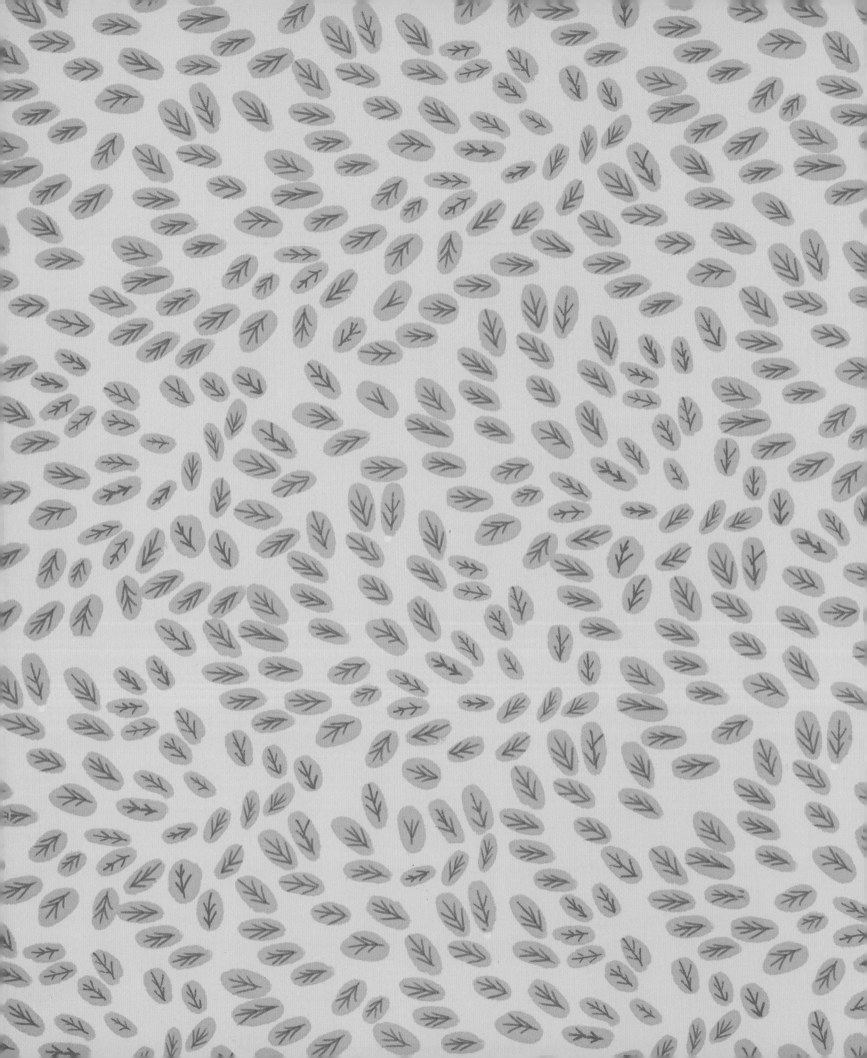

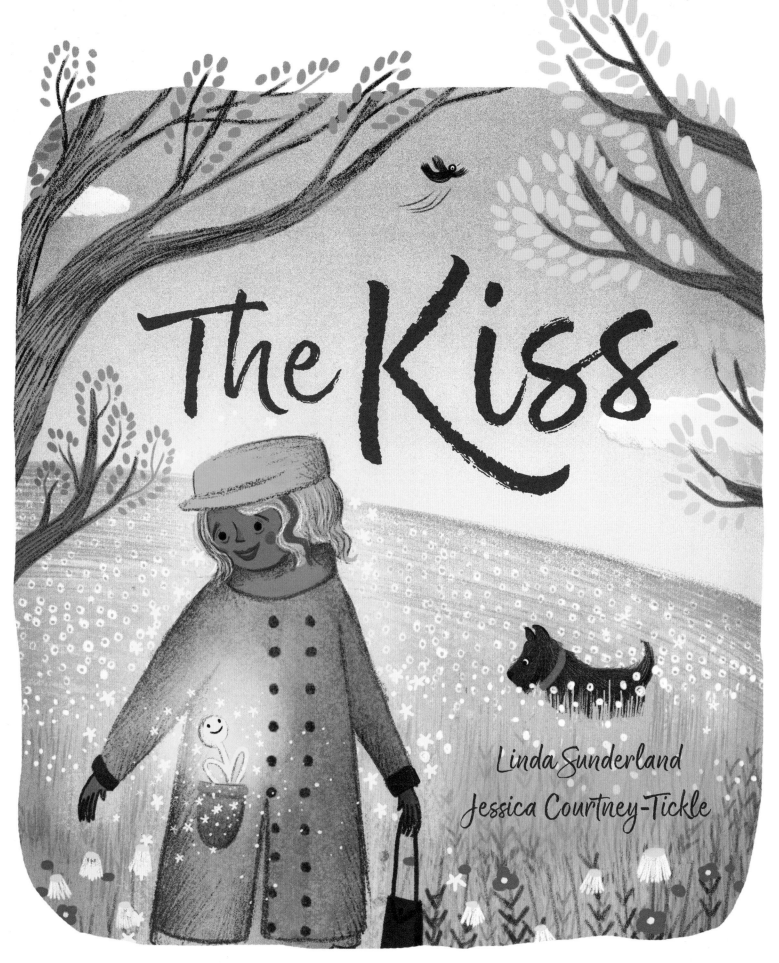

# The Kiss

Linda Sunderland

Jessica Courtney-Tickle

**LITTLE TIGER**

LONDON

Grandma was going home
from Edwyn's house.
Edwyn was busy playing with his
baby brother so he blew her a kiss.
She caught it and put it in her pocket.

At the bus stop, Grandma sat next to
an old man who looked sad.
She took the kiss from her pocket and showed it to him.

The old man smiled. Then he took Grandma's
hand and they began to dance.
Right there on the pavement.

The people at the bus stop smiled.

Then they danced too!
No one knows where
the music came from.

When the bus arrived, Grandma said goodbye
and blew the old man a kiss.
He caught it and put it in his pocket.
But she kept Edwyn's kiss safe.

Grandma got off the bus
and walked through the park.
A woman was shouting horrid
words at her little girl.

Grandma took the
kiss from her pocket
and showed it to the
shouty lady.

All the nasty, spiky words turned
into bright balloons that floated round
her head in clouds.
The lady and the little girl began to laugh.

Grandma noticed the kiss was getting heavier.
The more it was used, the bigger it got.

Back home, Grandma got a shock.
At her door was a man dressed in important clothes.
He'd parked his important car and blocked the road.
He smiled a smile too wide for his face.

He'd heard about the kiss and wanted to buy it.

"Why?" asked Grandma.

"Because I am so rich, I can have anything I want," said the man.

But Grandma would not sell the kiss.

Every day, the man came back. He brought Grandma flowers.

He dropped letters down her chimney.

He kept her awake
with a big brass band.
But still she would
not sell the kiss.

So he stole it from her.

The rich man took
the kiss to his tower
and put it inside a silver
cage so that only he
could see it.

But, day by day,
the kiss grew thinner.

The skies turned mean.

The sun went to sleep.

The kiss was fading inside its silver cage and the rich man grew sad.

He carried the silver cage
to Grandma's house.
Grandma made him a cup of tea.
She baked him lemon cake
and ginger snaps.

Then she opened the cage
and slipped the kiss back
into her pocket.

When the rich man was leaving, Grandma saw
how sad he was, so she blew him a kiss.

The man caught it and put it in his pocket.
He smiled a sweet happy smile, just the right size for his face.

The next time Grandma saw Edwyn,
he gave her a big hug.

She hung it in her wardrobe.
"That will keep me warm whenever
I feel cold or lonely," she said.

And she was right.

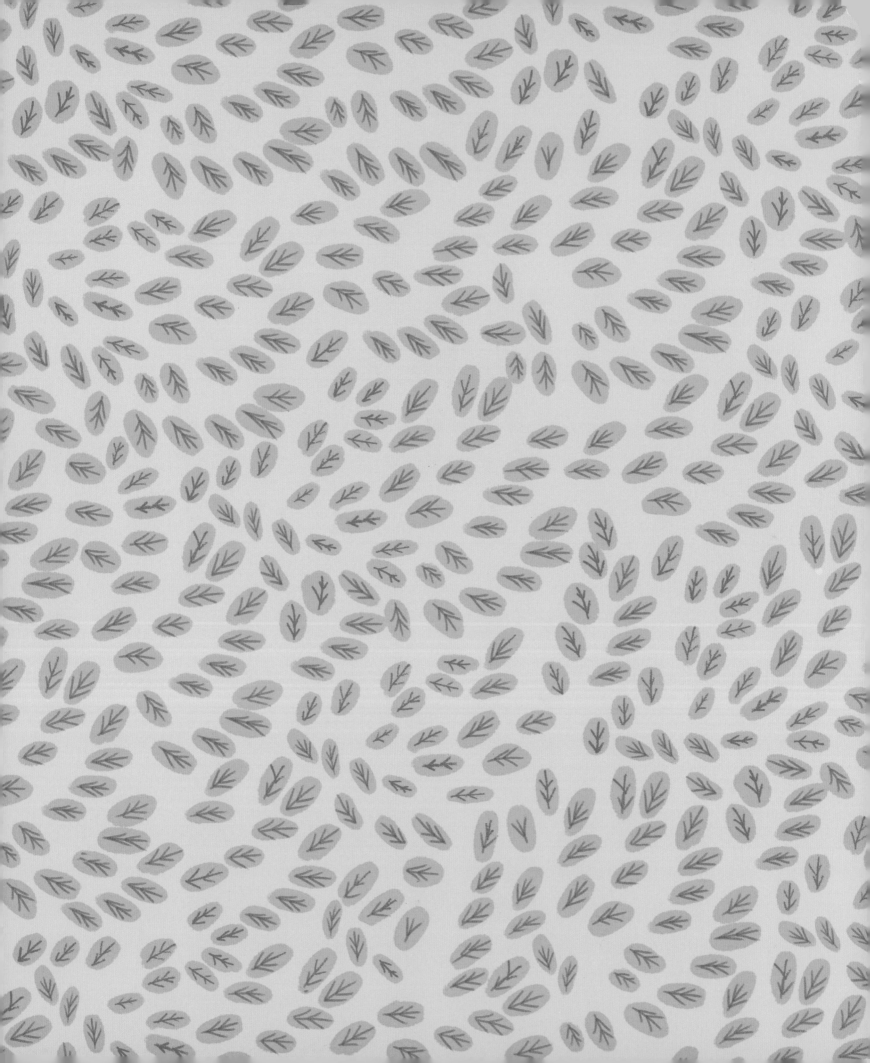

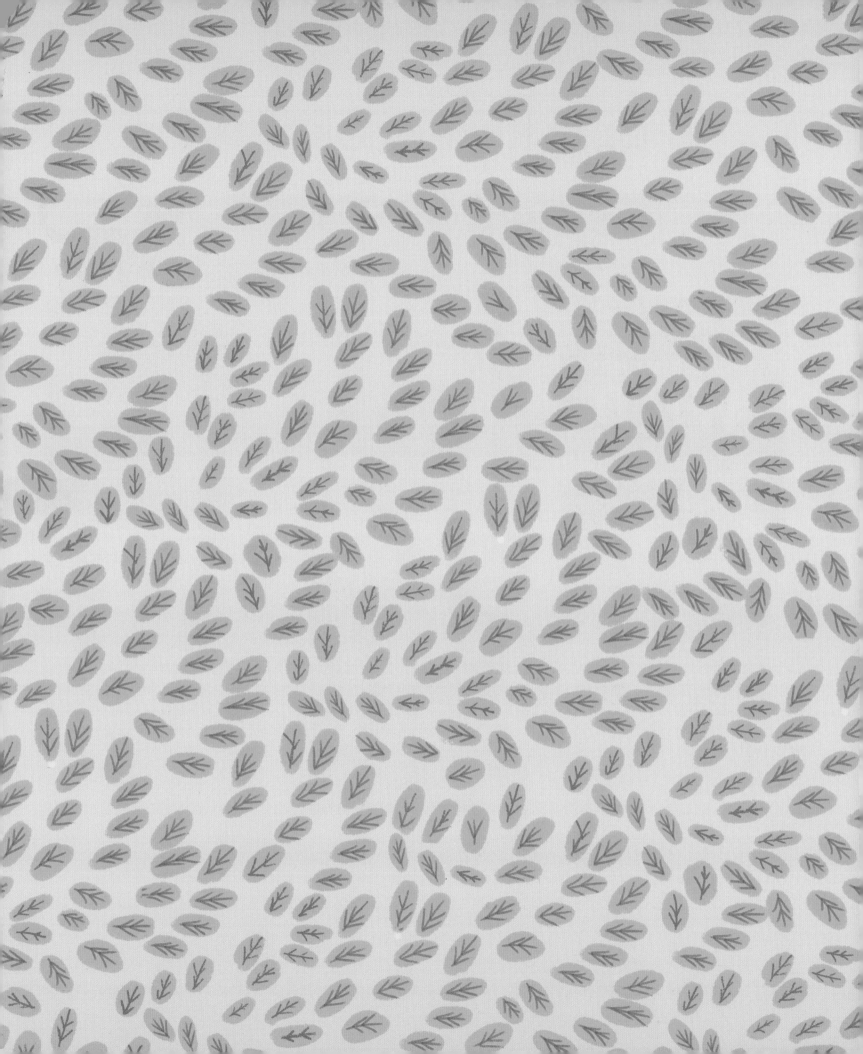

# More beautiful books from Little Tiger Press . . .

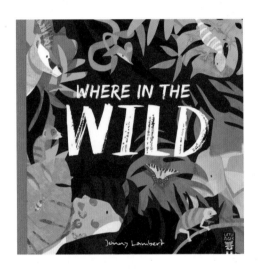

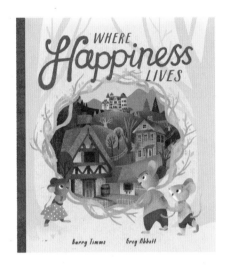

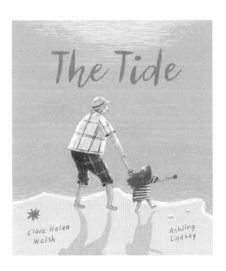

For information regarding any of the above titles or for our catalogue, please contact us:

Little Tiger Press Ltd, 1 Coda Studios, 189 Munster Road, London SW6 6AW

Tel: 020 7385 6333 • E-mail: contact@littletiger.co.uk • www.littletiger.co.uk